Nailed It

A Love Story in Progress

Antoinette T Burson

Nailed It
A Love Story in Progress
Love doesn't need a mansion—just room to bloom.

Printed in the United States of America
ISBN: 979-8-9938898-0-1 Paperback
ISBN: 979-8-9938898-1-8 E-book/Kindle

A Note from the Author

I wrote this story as part healing and part manifestation.

I'm 54 years old, and like many of you, I've lived a few lifetimes already — loved deeply, lost pieces of myself along the way, healed quietly, and slowly made my way back to joy.

And you know what I still believe, deep in my bones?

That I — we — deserve a second chance at love.

Not just the butterflies and flirty texts (although yes, please!), but the kind of love that sees you fully, holds your hand without dimming your light, and kisses you like you're still someone's favorite song.

This series follows three women — Nia, Tasha, and Simone — all over 40, all different, all navigating life, love, and healing in their own beautiful ways. Maybe you'll find yourself in one of them. Or maybe, like most of us, you'll see little pieces of yourself in all three.

Because we are multifaceted women.

We can be soft and strong.

Wild and wise.

Whole and still open.

Thank you for supporting my dream, for letting these stories live in your hands and hearts. And most of all, thank you for reminding me that we're never too old to choose love, build new beginnings, and write our own kind of happy ending.

I see you.

Because I am you.

With love,

Antoinette

Table of Contents

Introduction

This is a love story, but not the kind that starts with a whirlwind and ends with a white dress.

This is a grown love story.

The kind that comes after the dust has settled. After the heartbreak, the healing, the long nights of silence, and the slow mornings of figuring out who you are without the noise.

This is Nia's story. A woman who didn't give up on love but stopped chasing the version the world said she was supposed to want. She chose herself first. Built a life with her hands, her heart, and her faith. And when love showed up again, it wasn't loud. It was steady. It didn't come to rescue her. It came to join her.

She's not alone on this journey. Tasha and Simone — her business partners, her friends, her village — walk beside her. Each woman strong in her own way, each one creating a new kind of life in the Kentucky hills, surrounded by trees, truth, and possibility.

This is the first book in a series about second chances, tiny homes, deep kisses, and wide-open futures.

It's for every woman who knows her worth, who carries both

softness and fire, and who understands that love — real love — doesn't complete her.

It chooses her.

Every. Single. Day.

Chapter 1

A Life She Built with Her Own Hands

Nia's hands were in the dirt before the sun finished rising.

The Kentucky air was still cool, a soft mist clinging to the ground like the last sigh of a dream. Her fingers brushed over basil leaves, checking for pests, inhaling the scent of the fresh herbs. This was her favorite time of day, when everything was still, and she could hear herself think.

She leaned back on her heels and looked out over the land. Eleven acres. Eleven acres of possibility. The fruit trees were just starting to take, the herb beds were full, and the tomato vines looked promising. The greenhouse glowed in the distance, catching the early light like a quiet promise. It had taken time — so much time — but it was hers.

Well, theirs.

She smiled, thinking of Tasha and Simone. The three of them, out here trying to make something beautiful. A tiny home community where women like them — independent, soul-rich, done with settling — could grow and breathe. They weren't just building houses. They were creating their sanctuary.

Her phone buzzed beside her water bottle. A message from a coaching client:

"I finally told him no. Just like we practiced. I feel powerful."

Nia exhaled deeply, pride and peace wrapping around her like a shawl. Coaching women over 40 had become her calling. Helping them find joy again, helping them remember themselves. Because she knew what it was like to forget.

She'd forgotten once. In her marriage.

It wasn't that he was a bad man. He just didn't see her. Not really. Over the years, she became smaller and smaller until one day, she didn't recognize herself in the mirror. Divorce wasn't a heartbreak; it was a homecoming.

Now, at 54, she was finally her own woman. No one to answer to, no one to shrink for.

Still, if she was honest — and she always was with herself — there were nights when the wind moved through the trees just right, and a quiet ache settled in her chest. Not for what was, but for what could be.

Love wasn't a need. But the right love? That could be sweet.

If he had faith.

If he was kind.

If he met her spiritually, emotionally, physically.

If she could say everything in her heart and be held in it, not judged.
If he loved people. Loved animals. Loved deeply.

She chuckled softly. That was a unicorn list.

But then again, she was kind of a unicorn herself.

Wiping her hands on her jeans, she stood, stretched, and looked back toward the tiny house behind her. Nia's tiny home was clad in honey-toned cedar, soft and earthy like a sun-warmed path through the woods. The sage-green door stood as a quiet invitation, while the bronze accents gave it a touch of old-soul sophistication. Everything about it felt like her — grounded, intentional, and filled with peace. Her sanctuary. Her fresh start.

The kettle would be ready soon. She had lemon balm to steep and a day full of soil, sunshine, and sisterhood ahead.

And maybe, just maybe, something else waiting in the breeze.

Chapter 2

The Dream They're Building

"You know this solar panel ain't gonna install itself," Tasha called out, hands on her hips and brow glistening in the morning sun.

Nia looked up from the herb bed with a smirk. "Give me ten minutes. The basil was whispering to me."

Simone, in her wide-brimmed straw hat and lemon-print apron, wandered over with two mason jars of sweet tea. "Y'all arguing already and the day just got started. Lord, help us."

Tasha took her tea with a grateful nod and a wink. "Don't act like you're not gonna be posting this to the 'gram later with some *'women who build together, heal together'* caption."

"Guilty," Simone said with a little shrug. "But that doesn't make it untrue."

It had been just over a year since they broke ground on their dream. Eleven acres of Kentucky soil, three tiny homes in progress, and plans for more. The vision was simple: a self-sustaining tiny home community built by women, for women. A place for fresh starts, purpose, and peace.

Each woman brought her own magic to the land.

Tasha, with her toned arms and quiet intensity, was the builder. Solar panels, rain catchment systems, and compost toilets. She could build a wall, wire a light fixture, and break your heart with that half-smile of hers.

Simone, all Southern sparkle and digital savvy, had taken over branding, content creation, and online outreach. She filmed tutorials, managed their page, and had already built a small following of folks cheering them on from all over the country. *"Tiny Living with Big Heart,"* she'd dubbed it.

And Nia? Nia made things grow. From seedlings and squash to the quiet confidence in their collective spirit, she nurtured life. Her clients called her a joy coach, and it wasn't just a title. It was truth. Her presence soothed, even when she was deadpan roasting you about not labeling your herb jars.

This morning, the three women stood beneath the clear blue sky, laughing over tea, surrounded by the hum of bees and the slow dance of leaves in the breeze. Their work was physical, but the energy between them was light.

"So what's our next step after these last panels go in?" Simone asked, sipping her tea and eyeing the corner of the property where raised garden beds would eventually grow community veggies.

"Rain catchment barrels," Tasha said. "Then maybe we start on the shared kitchen."

Nia smiled, brushing a speck of dirt from her cheek. "And after that?"

Tasha glanced at her, then out at the horizon. "Then we breathe."

The three women stood quietly for a moment, listening to the land. No traffic, no drama, no demands. Just the low rustle of trees, the creak of wood, and the heartbeat of possibility.

"We're doing it," Simone said softly. "We're really building something."

Nia felt it too, deep in her chest. A sense of rightness. A chapter beginning.

They hadn't come here to be rescued.

They'd come to remember who they were — but also, who they were becoming.

Chapter 3

The Man at the Market

Nia wasn't looking for anything other than fresh peaches and a good price on goat cheese.

The Saturday market was buzzing. Families pushed strollers, musicians played old-school country, and the smell of kettle corn drifted through the warm air. She loved this little town more than she'd expected to. It wasn't flashy, but it felt solid. The kind of place where people remembered your name and asked about your dog, even if you didn't have one yet.

She reached for a basket of peaches when a deep voice caught her ear.

"No, ma'am, let me grab that for you."

Nia looked up instinctively. A man — tall, mid to late 50s maybe — was helping an older woman load a crate of tomatoes into her trunk. His sleeves were rolled up, arms toned and tanned. His voice had a quiet confidence to it. No bravado. Just kind.

The woman thanked him, and he gave a simple nod, like it was nothing.

Nia turned back to the peaches, but she felt it — that low buzz under her skin. The quiet ping of awareness.

She didn't stare. She wasn't thirteen, for goodness' sake.

But when she caught a glimpse of him again near the honey stand, she noticed more. Salt-and-pepper beard. A few tattoos peeking out from under his sleeve. And the way he greeted the vendor like they were old friends. She caught just enough of their conversation to hear something about a daughter visiting next month, and needing to clean up his porch.

He laughed, easy and full.

And Nia smiled to herself.

She didn't speak to him. Didn't even make eye contact. This wasn't a movie where they spot each other from across the room, she reminded herself with a little laugh. Too many romance books. Besides, for all she knew, he was married, or emotionally unavailable, or allergic to herbs. Who knew?

But as she made her way toward the car with her canvas bag in tow, she glanced back once more.

He was leaning over a table of handmade dog treats, talking to the vendor and pointing to a sign for local adoptions.

Her heart tugged, and she rolled her eyes at herself.

Calm down. It's just a man. Albeit a good-looking one.

Still… it had been a long time since she noticed anyone. Even longer since someone made her nervous without saying a word.

She buckled her seatbelt and rested her hands on the steering wheel, heart still just a little too quick.

Maybe it was nothing.

But maybe — just maybe — it was something.

Chapter 4

The Unexpected Spark

The café was quiet for a weekday. Nia preferred it that way—no long lines, no rushed orders, just the gentle hum of the espresso machine and the occasional soft laugh from someone enjoying their morning.

She was there for a refill of her favorite blend: dark roast, a hint of cinnamon, and a moment to read over client notes before her next virtual session. She sat by the window, laptop open, glasses sliding slightly down her nose—completely in her element.

Until she heard that voice again.

"I think I saw you at the market last weekend," he said casually, stepping up beside her table with a coffee in hand.

She looked up.

It was him.

The peach stand man. Sleeves rolled up again. That salt-and-pepper beard. Those same calm eyes that saw people—not just past them.

"Oh," Nia said, a little too quickly. "Maybe. I go every Saturday."

He smiled, warm and easy. "I was there helping Ms. Gentry with her tomatoes. She said the peaches were the sweetest they'd been in years, so I went to check them out. Saw you holding one up like you were about to give it a grade."

Nia chuckled. "I take my fruit seriously."

"You and me both. I don't play about a good peach." He gave her a wink, then lifted his cup. "Mind if I sit?"

She hesitated just long enough to feel the heat rise in her cheeks, then nodded, trying to play it cool. "Sure."

He slid into the chair across from her—no tension, no awkward energy. Just his presence.

"I'm Eli," he said, reaching across the table.

Nia took his hand—firm shake, warm skin. "Nia."

They had an easy, genuine conversation. They talked about the market, the land she lived on with her friends, and his favorite trails nearby. He asked thoughtful questions—not invasive, but real. Like he was interested in more than small talk.

When she told him about the tiny house project, he leaned in slightly. "That's impressive. Most people talk about simplifying but never actually do it."

"We didn't want to wait for the perfect time," she said. "We just wanted to live on purpose—now."

He nodded, like he got it. "That's beautiful."

She noticed the tattoo on his forearm then—a tree with roots wrapping around scripture numbers. She didn't ask, but it stayed in her mind long after.

They didn't exchange numbers. There was no flirty banter, no pressure. Just a connection—easy and steady, like the first breeze of a new season.

As she walked back to her car, she realized she was smiling—the kind of smile that crept up before you could stop it.

She hadn't felt this... seen in a long time.

She didn't know if he'd show up again.

But if he did?

She wouldn't mind at all.

Chapter 5

Show Up and Offer Help

Eli hadn't stopped thinking about her since the café.

Not in a teenage-crush kind of way. It was quieter than that—more settled. Like the feeling you get when you walk into a room and everything just feels right.

She was... grounded. That's what struck him first. The way she carried herself, like she wasn't performing for anyone. Comfortable in her own skin—but not arrogant about it. Just calm and confident.

He liked that she didn't flirt. Liked that she didn't try to fill the silence with empty words. She listened—really listened. And when she spoke, it was with intention. That kind of woman was rare. And by this point in life, most men had stopped believing she existed.

He'd dated since his divorce—nothing serious. Most of the time, it fizzled. A lot of surface-level charm but not much depth. And honestly, he was fine on his own. He had his home, his daughter, his quiet routines. But Nia stirred something in him that wasn't loud or needy—just curious.

And curiosity had him driving out toward the edge of town,

past tall sycamores and winding gravel, toward the land he'd heard whispers about.

Three women building a tiny home community from scratch. Most folks in town thought it was "a cute idea" or "some Instagram thing," but he knew better. He could tell by Nia's hands—calloused and sun-kissed. That wasn't online cute. That was real work.

He pulled up slowly and parked near what looked like a work shed. The land was peaceful. Young fruit trees in neat rows. Raised beds full of greens. A few chickens scratching near a wire fence. Toward the back, a small cedar house caught his eye. It looked like the kind of home built by someone who cared about every detail.

He stepped out just as she rounded the corner, a coil of hose in her hand and a bandana tied around her head.

Her eyes widened slightly in surprise, then softened. "Eli?"

He gave a half smile, one hand in his pocket. "Hope I'm not overstepping. I was out this way and thought I'd come see what you're building. Small town—it wasn't too hard to find you."

She blinked, then gave a small, quiet laugh. "You just happened to be out this way, huh?"

"Maybe I got curious," he said. "Maybe I wanted to see if you were really living what you talked about."
Maybe I just needed to see that smile again, he thought. He didn't realize how much until he pulled into her drive.

She nodded, then gestured toward the shed. "We're in the middle of reinforcing the roof. One good storm and it might end up in the neighbor's pasture."

He looked up at it, then back at her. "I've got a drill and two hands."

Nia arched an eyebrow. "You always show up with unsolicited manual labor?"

"Only when I'm impressed," he said simply.

She stared at him a moment longer, then smiled—slow,

reluctant, but real.

"Alright then. Let's see what you've got."

And just like that, he fell into rhythm beside her. No pressure. No flirtation. Just shared work, shared silence, and the quiet beginning of something neither of them saw coming.

But both felt it.

Chapter 6

The Way She Moves

Now finished with the shed's roof, she'd moved on to the next task.

Eli stood with one hand resting on a beam of the shed, watching Nia haul a heavy bag of compost toward the garden beds.

She moved with purpose—no hesitation, no complaints. Just quiet strength and the kind of grace that didn't know it was being watched.

Does she even know how good she looks like that? he thought. Sweat beading at her temple, curls tucked under a bandana, loose tank top clinging just enough to suggest the softness beneath. Strong and sunlit—without even trying.

"You're gonna throw your back out," he called, stepping closer.

Nia didn't stop. "Only if I lift with my ego."

He laughed, deep and surprised. "Fair enough."

She reached the edge of the raised bed and dropped the bag with a satisfied grunt. "You here to supervise or lend a hand?"

"Little of both," he said, picking up a shovel. Eli glanced around, taking it all in—the cedar house, the garden beds, the quiet care in every detail.

"You're really doing something out here," he said. "Something honest. I admire that."

Nia looked over at him, one brow raised. "You say that like it's rare."

He gave a small shrug. "Well... it is."

He paused, then added, "A lot of people love the idea of this kind of life. But you're living it. That takes grit."

There was a beat of silence while they worked—digging, mixing, turning soil. The rhythm of the task settled between them. No need to fill every space with talk.

Still, he couldn't help himself.

"You make this land look good, Nia."

She looked up, surprised. "What?"

He shrugged, not hiding the smile tugging at the corners of his mouth. "Just an observation. You out here, all focused and in your element. It suits you."

Nia chuckled softly and bent to adjust a trellis, her voice quieter now. "It's not every day someone calls me beautiful while I'm knee-deep in compost."

"I didn't say beautiful," he said, stepping closer. "I said you make this land look good."

She rolled her eyes, but her smile stayed. "Same thing."

"Almost," he said. Then added gently, "But since you brought it up... yeah. You are."

She froze for a split second—not in discomfort, but in that startled way a woman pauses when someone sees her too clearly. Then she stood, dusting off her hands.

"Well," she said, a small smile tugging at her lips, "guess I've been more transparent than I thought."

He shook his head slowly. "No. You're just finally being seen."

Another silence stretched between them. It wasn't awkward. It was thick—with unspoken questions, curiosity, and the tiniest curl of anticipation.

Nia finally broke it with a smirk. "Come on, you said you had two hands. Let's see what else you can lift."

Eli grinned, grabbing another bag and falling into step beside her.

And just like that, they got back to work—side by side, soil under their nails, a little sweat on their skin... and something growing between them.

Not exactly sure what.

But it was there.

And it was the beginning of something beautiful.

Chapter 7

Firelight and Friendship

The fire pit crackled softly, casting a warm glow across the yard as dusk settled into night. Fireflies blinked in the distance—the kind of magic that only showed up when you were still enough to notice.

Tasha leaned back in one of the camp chairs, balancing a plate of roasted veggies on her thigh.

"Simone, if you try to make me join that dating app one more time, I swear—"

Simone waved her off dramatically. "I'm just saying, your solar panel game is top tier, but your dating life could use a little... spark."

"I've got sparks," Tasha said. "Just not the kind that come with monthly subscriptions. More like the kind that come with batteries."

Nia laughed, her head thrown back, curls catching the firelight. Eli watched her from across the circle, his plate forgotten in his lap. That laugh—it was everything. Joyful. Free. Like someone who had earned her peace and knew how to enjoy it.

He hadn't planned on staying for dinner. But after a few hours helping Nia reinforce the shed and fix a stubborn window crank, Simone had come outside with a pitcher of something citrusy and iced, declaring, "You're not leaving without food. It's a rule."

Now he was here, full from grilled vegetables and spiced lentil patties, sipping something cold and tangy, and feeling... strangely at home.

"You alright over there, Eli?" Simone asked with a sly grin.

He blinked, caught. "Yeah. Just enjoying the show."

Nia glanced over at him, that soft, knowing smile tugging at her lips.

"These two always like this?" he asked, nodding at Simone and Tasha.

"Only on days ending in Y," Nia said.

The women laughed, and Eli felt something settle in his chest— not just attraction, not just admiration. It was something deeper. A sense of rightness. Like this was a table he could sit at. A life he could step into.

He leaned slightly toward Nia, voice low so only she could hear. "You're even more beautiful when you're comfortable."

She looked at him, startled for a moment—not because of the compliment, but because of how genuinely it landed.

"Thank you for that. I don't always feel beautiful," she admitted, eyes flickering toward the fire.

"Well," he said, eyes steady on hers, "you should."

She held his gaze longer than she meant to, her breath catching just slightly before she turned back to the others. The fire cracked again, loud in the sudden quiet.

Tasha cleared her throat. "Alright now, if you two are about to get all rom-com, I need to grab another drink."

Simone giggled, standing up with her glass. "Same. Let the grown folks flirt. We'll give you a five-minute head start."

Nia shook her head, smiling, as the two women walked toward

Simone's tiny house. Eli stayed quiet, letting the silence speak.

Finally, she looked at him.

"Thanks for staying."

He shrugged, voice soft. "Thanks for having me. I like it here."

She nodded. "Yeah. Me too."

The fire popped again, sending sparks into the night sky.

And for a moment, everything felt exactly as it should.

Chapter 8

Tasha Talks Real

The air was cooler this morning, and the clouds rolled in low and soft, wrapping the land in a muted hush.

Nia stood near the edge of the solar shed, coiling a length of wire that Tasha had cut. They were doing maintenance on the battery bank—a job that Nia mostly assisted with by passing tools and listening to Tasha explain things in her steady, no-nonsense way.

But today, Tasha was quieter than usual. Focused, but also somewhere else.

"You okay?" Nia asked, wiping her hands on a towel.

Tasha nodded, then paused. "Yeah. Just... been thinking."

Nia waited. With Tasha, you didn't rush the talk. You made space for it.

After a moment, Tasha stood up and stretched, her tank top rising just enough to reveal the tattoo on her lower side—a small heart with a date etched into it. The miscarriage. The baby that never got to be.

"I had a dream last night," she finally said. "About him. Marcus."

Nia's heart softened. She didn't say anything—just stepped closer, her presence a quiet yes.

"In the dream, we were laughing. Just sitting in the car like we used to, radio low, windows down. And I reached over to touch his leg... and my hand went right through him."

Nia swallowed. "Tash..."

"It wasn't sad," she said quickly. "Not really. It felt like... closure. Like I could finally let go of the guilt."

They stood in silence, the wind brushing past them like a whisper.

"I'm okay—better, Nia," Tasha said after a moment. "But sometimes I wonder if healing made me... guarded."

"Guarded or wise?"

Tasha smiled, a little sad. "Maybe both."

She turned to face Nia fully now. "You like this man, huh?"

Nia hesitated, then nodded. "Yeah. I do."

Tasha studied her, eyes sharp but kind. "Does he see you?"

"I think so."

"You want him to?"

That question hit harder than she expected. Nia looked away, chewing her bottom lip.

"I want someone who chooses me," she said softly. "Without games. Without needing to dim my light or shrink myself just to keep him."

"And if he sees all of you—your joy, your fire, your softness—are you ready to be wanted like that?"

Nia met her gaze, breath catching. "I don't know."

Tasha smiled, and it was the most tender thing in the world. "That's the thing about wanting real love, Nia. You gotta be ready to receive it—not just hope for it."

She reached over and gave Nia's arm a gentle squeeze. "It's okay to want the kind that makes you feel... full. Desired. Chosen."

Nia nodded slowly, feeling something unravel and settle inside her all at once.

Tasha turned back toward the batteries and picked up her wrench. "Now hand me that voltage meter before I say something else deep and make us both cry."

Nia laughed, blinking back the tears that were definitely not falling. "Bossy."

"Damn right."

And just like that, they were back to wiring and work—but Nia's heart was beating louder than before.

Chapter 9

The Town Fair

"You sure you wanna do this?" Nia asked herself, brushing imaginary dust off her sundress as she stepped out of her truck and walked up to meet Eli.

Eli was already waiting by the gate, two tickets in hand and a smile that was too easy on the eyes. "You afraid of funnel cake or Ferris wheels?"

"I'm not afraid of either," she said, walking up beside him. "But this feels dangerously close to a date."

He grinned, offering her a ticket. "What if I said I hoped it was?"

Nia arched a brow, but she took the ticket. "Then I guess I'd need to buy new lip gloss."

Eli laughed, deep and easy. "You don't need lip gloss, Nia. You don't need anything."

They walked into the fair together, shoulder to shoulder, both acting more casual than they felt. It had been years since she'd done something like this—something light, something just-for-fun. Something like going on a date. She didn't realize how much she'd missed it.

The place was full of local charm—string lights overhead,

booths selling kettle corn and handmade soaps, the clink of rings hitting milk bottles, kids running with snow cones.

"Let's make a deal," Eli said, glancing at her as they passed the corndog stand. "You win me a prize at ring toss, and I'll buy you the best sweet tea in the county."

Nia tilted her head. "You sure about that? I don't play to lose."

"I'm counting on it."

Ten minutes later, he was holding a small stuffed fox she insisted he had to carry, and she was sipping sweet tea with crushed ice and a hint of mint. Her cheeks hurt from smiling, and her heart... well, it was doing something new. Something fluttery.

They wandered toward the animal area, neither of them saying much now. Just walking slow. Easy.

And then they saw her.

A small booth labeled **"Rescue Me"** stood under a big tree. Inside, a medium-sized mutt—wiry fur, honey-brown eyes, and the gentlest face—sat quietly while other dogs barked and jumped around her.

Nia stopped. "Well, hey there," she said softly, kneeling in front of the pen.

The dog tilted her head, ears perked. Then she moved forward and sat right at the gate.

"She's choosing you," Eli murmured.

Nia looked up. "Don't tempt me."

"I'm not," he said, crouching beside her. "But if I were that dog, I'd pick you too."

She laughed, cheeks flushing as she turned back toward the pup. "Are you always this smooth?"

"What can I say—you bring it out of me."

They spent the next twenty minutes filling out forms, chatting with the rescue coordinator, and introducing the dog to her new name—Junie.

As they walked back toward the exit, Junie trotting beside them with her tongue hanging out like she'd just won the lottery, Nia bumped Eli's shoulder.

"So," she said, her tone light but curious, "does this count as meeting the family?"

Eli smiled, warm and full of something real. "Well then, I guess it's only fair I take you out for a proper dinner date."

She glanced at him, then ahead at the lights twinkling above the crowd.

And for the first time in a long time, Nia wasn't just hopeful.

She was open.

Chapter 10

Simone's Porch Wisdom

The morning after the fair was still and golden—the kind of soft summer morning that made everything feel like it was happening in slow motion.

Nia sat on Simone's porch with a steaming mug of lemon balm tea in hand, Junie curled at her feet like she'd always belonged there. The pup had slept like a rock, tail occasionally thumping against the wall of the tiny house in her dreams.

Simone walked out barefoot, two slices of toasted sourdough balanced on a napkin and her hair piled on top of her head in a messy bun.

"Well, well, well," she said, sliding into the chair beside Nia. "Look who came home with a man and a dog."

Nia rolled her eyes, trying not to smile. "It was not like that."

Simone handed her a slice of toast and settled in with her own tea. "You're glowing. Don't even fight me on it."

Nia sighed and gave in, laughing under her breath. "It was a good night."

"Mmm." Simone sipped her tea. "So, tell me... how'd it feel when he called you beautiful?"

Nia blinked, caught off guard. "How'd you know he said that?"

"I know the look," Simone said, tilting her head. "The one where your heart flinches a little, like it doesn't know whether to accept the compliment or file it away in case it's taken back later."

Nia didn't answer right away. She just looked out at the garden beds glistening with morning dew.

"I didn't know how much I needed to hear it until he said it."

"Of course you needed it. You're a woman, not a machine. We can love ourselves all day long—affirmations, self-care, journals, all of it—but it still feels different when it comes from someone who sees us."

Nia looked down at her tea. "He's... gentle. Present. And when he looks at me, it's like he's not seeing what I do, but something deeper."

Simone leaned in, voice dropping just enough to be serious. "And are you ready for that?"

"I think so," Nia said softly. "But it scares me a little."

"It should," Simone said. "Because it's real. And after a lifetime of settling or shrinking or being too much or not enough, real feels... unsteady. But it's also where the good stuff lives."

They sat quietly for a moment, sipping tea while Junie snored at their feet.

Then Simone nudged her gently with her elbow. "Just promise me one thing."

"What's that?"

"If this man keeps showing up for you, the way a real one does, promise me you won't disappear on him. Don't downplay your light. Don't act like you don't want to be chosen. Because sweet pea... you are the prize."

Nia smiled, slow and sure, her heart tugging in that way it did when something hit too close to the truth.

"Okay," she said. "I promise."

"Good," Simone replied, standing and stretching. "Now go write in that fancy journal of yours about how fine your man looked at the fair. I know you were staring."

Nia burst into laughter—the kind that spilled out like sunlight.

She looked down at Junie, who opened one sleepy eye and wagged her tail once.

Yeah. Life was getting sweeter by the day.

Chapter 11

The Slow Dance in the Kitchen

Eli arrived with a knock that was firm but unhurried, just like him.

Nia opened the door, apron tied at her waist, a wisp of steam curling from the kitchen behind her. "You came hungry, right?"

"I knew better than to eat before I got here," he said, stepping inside with a pie box and a slight smile. "And I brought dessert. Blackberry crisp from Mrs. Penny's stand."

"That'll buy you about thirty minutes of small talk," Nia said with a wink, taking the pie and motioning him toward the kitchen. "After that, I expect real conversation."

He followed, Junie padding behind them both like she'd appointed herself official hostess.

The table was already set. Rustic pottery plates, mismatched glasses, a sprig of lavender in an old jelly jar. Dinner was her usual garden magic: roasted potatoes with fresh dill, caramelized carrots, sautéed kale with lemon and garlic and salmon cooked over the fire.

They talked between bites about how the tomatoes were finally coming in, a neighbor's goat who kept escaping, the podcast

Simone wanted them to start. Their conversation had an easy rhythm. Familiar.

After dinner, Nia stood at the sink rinsing dishes while Eli dried. Music played low from the speaker, soft, soulful. Donny Hathaway maybe. Or early Sade.

When the next song drifted in, slow, smooth, the kind that wrapped around you like heat, Eli turned toward her.

"Dance with me."

There was a quiet pull in his voice, not loud or demanding, but steady... certain. The kind of certainty that made her pause, just for a breath, and feel it settle low in her chest.

Nia handed him the last plate, the clink of ceramic soft against the silence that had stretched between them all evening, tender and full.

She pulled the towel gently from his hands and set it aside without a word.

When she looked up, he was already stepping in, close enough for her to feel the warmth of him, the way his presence shifted the very air.

His hand found hers, fingers lacing like it was nothing new. His other hand landed at the small of her back, sure and warm, guiding.

And she let him.

The first few steps were slow, unhurried. The world narrowed to the sound of the music, the rhythm of their feet, the steady thrum of something unspoken blooming between them.

He didn't speak.

He didn't have to.

Nia's heart beat harder in her chest, not from nerves—but from the weight of being seen, held, wanted. Not rushed. Not pursued for sport.

Held.

His thumb brushed lightly over the back of her hand, and she swore it lit a fuse beneath her skin.

"You feel good in my arms," he murmured, low and close to her ear, his breath warming the skin of her neck.

She didn't answer right away. She didn't need to.

Her body leaned in a little more. Her fingers tightened around his. Her eyes fluttered shut for just a moment.

Letting herself feel it.

Letting herself want.

And right then, she knew, this was no casual dance.

This was a slow surrender.

They moved like they'd done it before in another life. No words, just warmth, bodies swaying, hearts settling into something unspoken.

He watched her, the way her lashes rested gently against her cheeks, the way she smiled without showing teeth.

"What are you thinking about?" she asked softly, not breaking the moment.

He didn't answer right away. Just kept moving with her, a sheepish smile like he'd been caught.

Then he said, low and deliberate, "I'm thinking I didn't know peace could have a scent... but right now, it smells like lemon balm and you."

Nia blinked.

Her heart didn't skip a beat, it settled deeper into her chest.

She looked up at him, eyes wide but steady. "That's a line."

"It's the truth," he said.

And the way he said it?

She believed him.

They didn't kiss, not yet.

But something passed between them in that small kitchen, under dim light and slow melody. Something that tasted like yes and felt like home.

Chapter 12

Seeds and Surprises

It had been a few weeks since that almost-kiss, and though the moment still lingered in her mind like a favorite song, chores didn't wait, not even for slow-burning feelings. She needed to swing by the garden co-op for a few things before heading back to the homestead.

Nia was standing at the garden co-op, comparing two nearly identical packets of cucumber seeds, when she heard his voice—smooth, low, familiar.

"I'm telling you, if you tasted her roasted carrots, you'd swear off restaurants for a year."

She turned her head, and sure enough, there he was, Eli, smiling as he walked through the door with a young woman beside him. She was tall, with copper-toned curls and sharp eyes that scanned the room before they even landed on Nia.

"Speak of the woman herself," Eli said as he approached. "Nia, what are the odds?"

Nia tucked the seed packets in her basket and smiled. "Higher than you think. This place is my second home."

Eli motioned to the young woman beside him. "This is my

daughter, Maya. Maya, this is Nia—the woman who grows food that makes grown men reconsider their life choices."

Nia stepped forward laughing and extended her hand. "It's a pleasure to meet you, Maya. Your father's mentioned you more than once."

Maya shook her hand, eyes still watchful but curious. "He's mentioned you, too. You're the one building a farm in the woods with two other women?"

"Tiny homes, actually," Nia said warmly. "We just finished reinforcing the shared kitchen roof. I'd give us a solid B-plus for the work and an A for teamwork."

Maya cracked a small smile. "That's impressive. Most people talk about simplifying, few actually do it."

"Sounds like something I would say," Eli chimed in.

"Because you did say it," Maya and Nia shot back, then Maya turned to Nia. "He's clearly a fan."

Nia chuckled. "The feeling's mutual."

The air softened after that. They talked for a few more minutes, Maya asking sharp, thoughtful questions about sustainability and community-building. She didn't miss a beat, but there was a quiet respect building in her tone.

Nia answered each question with her usual calm, not defensive, not self-important. Just natural. Grounded. Open.

At one point, Maya glanced at Eli and said, "You finally met someone who can keep up."

Nia smiled, "He's not too bad at keeping up himself."

Eli chuckled, rubbing the back of his neck.

When they wrapped up, Maya reached out and gently touched Nia's arm. "It was really nice to meet you."

"You too," Nia said, sincere. "Anytime you want to come see the land, just say the word. We've always got room at the table."

As they walked away, Junie trotted out from under the truck

and bumped Nia's leg with her nose.

"You heard that, didn't you?" Nia said softly, crouching to scratch behind her ears. "What do you think Junie girl? I think we're off to a good start." And with that, Junie gave a quick bark in agreement.

Later that night, a text came in from Eli:

"Maya said you're solid. Said you're someone she'd want on her team. That's rare for her."

Nia stared at the message for a moment before typing back:

"That means more than you know. Tell her I said thank you—and that the door's always open."

Chapter 13

The Ex Shows Up

The weeks that followed were slow and sweet, text messages, shared meals, quiet moments that stitched their lives a little closer together. When Nia mentioned the sustainability workshop, she hadn't expected Eli to say, "I'd love to go with you." But he did, and the warmth in his voice lingered with her all week.

It was a Saturday and the university greenhouse was buzzing with conversation and the earthy scent of freshly turned soil. Nia stood near a raised bed demo, listening intently as the instructor talked through compost layering and companion planting. She took notes quickly, mentally calculating how she could scale this for their land back home.

Eli leaned in earlier and whispered, "You could teach this," before heading off to the restroom. She smiled to herself at the memory, grateful he saw her that clearly.

She was flipping her page when she heard it, low and uncertain, but familiar.

"Nia?"

She turned and felt a beat of surprise. Jackson.

Her ex-husband stood a few feet away, a university badge

clipped to his shirt, one hand loosely in his pocket. Still clean-cut, still walking like the world owed him ease. But something was different, a little more gray at the temples, a little less arrogance in his shoulders.

"Jackson," she said, steady. Not cold, just... centered.

He stepped closer. "Someone mentioned a tiny house community outside of town, and I figured if anyone had something to do with it, it'd be you."

She raised an eyebrow, amused. "Never figured you for the composting workshop type."

He chuckled, a little sheepish. "Short-term consulting contract. Facilities design. The irony isn't lost on me."

His eyes lingered a moment, a little too long.

"You look... good," he added. "Different."

Nia didn't flinch. "It's called peace. Looks good on everyone."

That pulled a short breath from him. "I deserved that."

She tilted her head but said nothing.

He scratched the back of his neck, hesitating. "I've had a lot of time to think about things. And I just, I wanted to say I'm sorry. For how I showed up back then. For making you feel like you had to shrink just so we'd fit."

Her lips parted, but the words didn't come right away. "That was a long time coming. I appreciate you saying it."

Just then, a warm touch settled at the small of her back.

Eli.

She didn't even need to turn, she felt him, calm and sure.

She looked up at Jackson. "Jackson, this is Eli."

Jackson offered a nod, reading the moment clearly. "Nice to meet you."

Eli returned the nod with a polite one of his own.

Jackson cleared his throat. "Well... I'm glad I ran into you. I think maybe we both needed that closure."

Nia gave a small smile. "Maybe we did."

He gave her one last look, then turned and blended back into the crowd.

They stood in silence for a moment until Eli leaned in slightly, voice low. "You okay?"

She nodded, eyes on the greenhouse rows. "I am. I really am."

He didn't press, just stayed close, his presence solid and warm beside her.

And with her hand brushing lightly against his, Nia felt it again. Not the past pulling her back, but the future gently calling her forward.

Chapter 14

Porch Talk Under the Stars

The stars had come out bold that night.

Nia sat on her porch, legs tucked beneath her, a warm throw draped over her lap and a mug of lemon balm tea in her hands. Junie was stretched out near her feet, tail occasionally twitching in a dream.

The run in had been hours ago, but Jackson's sudden reappearance still lingered in the back of her mind. Not painfully, just faint like a bruise that no longer hurt but reminded you how far you'd come.

She heard footsteps on the gravel before she saw him.

Eli walked up carrying a thermos and two small tin mugs. "Didn't want to leave you with your thoughts tonight," he said.

Nia smiled, shifting slightly to make room. "Very thoughtful of you."

He handed her a mug. "Mint and ginger. Thought you might need something grounding."

She took a sip, warm and spicy. "You have a thing for showing up with good timing."

"I have a thing for showing up where I'm wanted."

She let the quiet hang between them for a moment, the stars blinking overhead like they were listening in.

"You handled that moment with your ex today..." Eli said as they sat, the evening air warm and breezy.

He looked over at her, steady. "You carried yourself with so much grace."

Nia let out a soft breath. "Thank you. I didn't expect to see him."

"You okay?"

She nodded, thoughtful. "I am. Honestly... it felt good, in a way. To see him, to hear him say the words I didn't even know I'd been waiting on."

Eli stayed quiet, giving her space.

"I lost myself in that marriage," she continued. "Piece by piece. Not because he was cruel or careless. Just... because I didn't know better back then. I didn't know how to hold onto me."

"And now?" he asked.

She looked over at him, a gentle smile tugging at the corner of her mouth. "Now, I do."

He reached over and brushed his thumb along the back of her hand. "Closure's a powerful thing."

"Yeah," she said quietly. "It is."

They sat in the silence between them, not heavy, but full, like a chapter finally closing.

And something new, quietly beginning.

She looked over at him. "You ever feel like... you became who you are after everything fell apart?"

"All the time," he said. "My marriage didn't end with a bang. It just... faded. But somewhere in all that silence, I realized I'd stopped being seen."

Nia sipped her tea, eyes steady on his. "Same."

He reached over, gently running a thumb across her knuckles. "I see you, Nia. In every way."

She looked at his hand on hers. "You sure about that? Because seeing me means seeing the whole story. My strength and the moments I still question everything. The quiet loneliness. The scars I don't always show."

"I don't want the edited version," he said, his voice steady. "I want all of it. All of you."

The breeze picked up just enough to rustle the trees, and the stars above them shimmered like they approved.

"I've spent a long time building a life that feels like mine," Nia said. "If someone's gonna be in it, I need them to stand beside me. Not try to fix me, or save me, or soften me to make me easier to hold."

Eli leaned in, his voice low. "I'm not here to soften you. I'm here to honor the weight you carry."

Nia blinked, throat tight.

She didn't cry. She'd shed enough tears.

But she felt something shift, deep and quiet, like the sound of a lock turning.

Chapter 15

Kiss Me Like You Mean It

The stars hadn't moved, but the world felt different.

They sat in comfortable silence, still on the porch, hands occasionally brushing as they passed the thermos back and forth. Junie was fast asleep, curled up like she belonged to both of them now.

Nia leaned her head back and closed her eyes, letting the quiet wrap around her like a second skin. She wasn't tired, just present. Peaceful.

Eli studied her in that way he did, never possessive, never needy. Just... observant. Like he was learning her, piece by piece.

"You always this calm at night?" he asked gently.

"Not always," she said without opening her eyes. "But when I'm with someone who doesn't make me shrink, I settle."

He smiled, slow and full. "You're something else, Nia."

She finally looked at him, with a soft smile. "You say that like you're just realizing that."

"No," he said, leaning slightly closer. "I noticed it the first time I saw you hold a peach like it was sacred. I've just been catching up ever since."

Her laugh was soft, a little breathy. And in that moment, her eyes didn't just meet his, they invited him in.

He reached for her hand, then ran a thumb over her wrist like he was memorizing the beat of her pulse. "Can I ask you something?"

"You just did."

He smirked. "Smart mouth."

She lifted a brow. "You like it."

"I do," he said, then sobered. "But I'm not trying to make a move just to say I did. If I kiss you… I want it to mean something."

Nia sat up straighter, her voice low. "Then kiss me like you mean it."

No hesitation.

Eli leaned in slowly, not because he wasn't sure, but because he was. He touched her cheek first, the pad of his thumb brushing just below her bottom lip, like he wanted to know what her quiet felt like.

And then he kissed her.

Soft at first.

Then deeper.

Not rushed.

Not testing.

Meaningful, passionate, wanting. Two people who had nothing to prove and everything to offer.

When they pulled back, Nia didn't look away.

Neither did he.

"Well damn," she whispered, voice a little raspier than before.

Eli grinned. "Still good?"

She nodded once. "Better than good."

They didn't say more after that. There was no need. The air

between them was charged and calm all at once. The kind of quiet that only comes when two people are finally, fully ready.

And as Nia sat beside Eli, her fingers laced with his, Junie curled at their feet, and the stars still blinking overhead... she realized something.

This wasn't the start of a fairytale.

This was the next chapter of a real one.

And she was ready for all of it.

Chapter 16

Mornings After and Other Sacred Things

The sun crept in through the sheer curtains, warming the room with soft, honey-colored light.

Nia blinked awake slowly, her body still half-draped in sleep, her breath even. She stretched, one leg slipping out from under the blanket as Junie hopped onto the edge of the bed with a soft whine.

"I know," Nia mumbled, smiling. "He's not here."

Last night had ended just past midnight, with stars overhead and Eli's kiss still clinging to her lips like something sacred. He hadn't stayed and she hadn't expected him to. After the kiss, after the silence that followed, he'd touched her cheek again and with a quick kiss said, "I'll let you sleep on that."

She liked that about him.

He didn't rush.

Didn't push.

But oh, he lingered in the most delicious ways.

She pulled on her robe and padded into the kitchen, Junie's nails clicking softly behind her. As the kettle began to boil, Nia stood at the window overlooking the back garden. Her herbs were coming in full, basil, lemon balm, chives, each green bloom like its own little declaration.

She felt full too.

But also... aware.

That kiss had shifted something. Not in a way that made her unsure, but in a way that made her want.

She didn't want the idea of him. She wanted him. His hands. His steadiness. The way he saw her without needing to be convinced. The way he watched her, not just her body, but her being.

As she poured the hot water over her tea strainer, her phone buzzed on the counter.

Eli:

"Woke up thinking about your hands. Hope they're holding something warm this morning."

Nia smiled, heat rising low in her belly. She took her mug and stepped out onto the porch, wrapping the throw around her shoulders.

Nia:

"My hands are good. My lips well, they're good too."

The typing bubble appeared right away. Then disappeared.

Then came back.

Eli:

"There's something about you I can't shake. And I'm not trying to."

She exhaled slowly, setting her phone down beside her.

This wasn't a game.

This was two people standing on solid ground, with a slow fire building between them. A fire they were both finally ready to feed.

She sipped her tea, eyes watching the trees sway gently in the breeze, Junie curled at her feet.

The morning was quiet.

But inside her?

Something had just started humming.

Chapter 17

Girls' Night Out

The heels were on. The lip gloss was shining. And Simone had insisted on a spritz of something floral and flirty before they even left the driveway.

"You're glowing, sis," she said, tilting Nia's chin and giving a satisfied nod. "You trying to be subtle, but we see it."

"I'm just well-rested," Nia said with a small smirk.

"Mmhmm," Tasha added from the driver's seat. "That 'well-rested' look got a name and broad shoulders."

Nia rolled her eyes but didn't deny it. "We just kissed."

Simone gasped like she'd been personally robbed. "Just kissed?"

"And it was intentional," Nia added, more serious now. "Like, full eye contact, hands on my face, breath-stealing intentional."

Tasha whistled low. "Now that's a kiss."

The bar they pulled up to was small but stylish, tucked between a bookstore and a bakery that always smelled like cinnamon and dreams. Inside, a local blues band played on a low stage, and the lighting was just dim enough to make everyone look a little softer, a little finer.

They claimed a corner booth, ordered sparkling rosé and sweet potato fries, and let the laughter do what it does best, melt away whatever weight they'd been carrying.

"So what's the hold-up?" Simone asked between sips. "You're both single. You like each other. The spark is there."

Nia took her time before answering. "It's not a hold-up. It's a knowing. I want to be sure we're moving with intention, not just momentum."

Tasha nodded slowly. "You're not afraid of love. You're afraid of falling before he's ready to catch you."

"That part," Nia whispered, tracing the rim of her glass.

Simone leaned in. "Do you think he's scared?"

"I think he feels everything I feel," Nia said. "And that kind of clarity can be... a lot."

The band picked up a little, a low groove that moved through the room like honey. Tasha bopped her shoulders to the beat. Simone was already scanning the room for a dance partner. And Nia—Nia just sat back and let it all soak in.

This was her life now.

Soil and stars.

Sisterhood and slow kisses.

And the possibility of a love that matched her in depth, not just desire.

Simone grabbed her hand and pulled her up. "Come on, girl. You need to move that body. Shake off those thoughts and make some room for joy."

Nia laughed and let herself be led to the tiny dance floor, where they moved like they were in someone's backyard, barefoot and free.

And as she twirled under the amber lights, hair bouncing, arms open wide, Nia realized something simple but powerful:

She wasn't waiting for love to come find her.
She was already living in it.

Chapter 18

The Pullback

At first, it was small things.

A missed call.

A text reply that came hours later instead of minutes.

Plans for a Sunday lunch that turned into, "Raincheck? Something came up."

Nothing sharp. Nothing dramatic. Just... distance.

And Nia felt every inch of it.

She didn't panic. Didn't spiral. But she noticed.

Because when a man's energy had been steady, warm, consistent, thoughtful, the absence of that rhythm became its own kind of noise.

By Thursday, she sat on her porch with Junie stretched across her feet and a knot in her chest she hadn't expected. Not heartbreak. Just a quiet ache.

He hadn't ghosted. They still talked. But something felt off.

Eli wasn't leaning in anymore.

And Nia?

She refused to chase.

Her phone buzzed.

Eli:

"Been a long week. Can we catch up this weekend?"

She stared at the screen for a beat, then typed back:

Nia:

"Of course. Let me know what works for you."

She pressed send.

Then set her phone down, exhaled, and closed her eyes.

The weekend came, but he didn't.

Not really.

He showed up Saturday afternoon, well, not physically, just in the form of a short call. His voice was steady but distracted. He asked how her herbs were growing, laughed at a joke she made, but when she asked him how he was doing, his answer was too smooth.

"I'm good. Just tired. Just... thinking about stuff."

Nia paused.

"What kind of stuff?"

Eli was quiet on the other end. Then he said, "Life. Timing. Just... making sure I'm not moving too fast."

There it was.

The hesitation.

The fear.

She swallowed, not hurt, just disappointed. "Okay," she said softly.

"I don't want to mess this up," he added quickly. "I just need a little space to clear my head."

And Nia, because she knew what it meant to honor someone else's pace, and her own worth, replied, "Take what you need."

But the call ended with a weight she didn't like.

Not because he was pulling back.

But because she knew something he hadn't figured out yet:

Love isn't a risk when it's rooted.

It's a choice.

That night, she sat outside with a notebook and wrote a single line:

"I will not shrink just to fit into someone else's pause."

She underlined it twice.

And turned the page.

Chapter 19

Fire Pit Truths

The fire crackled low and steady, casting a warm glow against the dark velvet of the night. The sky was full. A soft spatter of stars stretching across the horizon like spilled sugar.

Simone passed Nia a glass of red wine and dropped into the chair beside her, wrapping a fleece blanket around her shoulders like a cloak.

"I made a playlist for tonight," she announced, pulling out a little Bluetooth speaker and pressing play. Nina Simone's voice floated out, low, smoky, full of meaning.

Nia took a slow sip and gave her a side-eye. "Is this a vibe check?"

"No," Simone said, settling deeper into the chair. "This is a soul check. Big difference."

Nia smirked but didn't argue. She knew exactly why Simone was here.

Tasha was off doing repairs on the water catchment system, giving them space. Simone had a way of knowing when someone needed quiet and when someone needed truth. And tonight?

Truth was on the menu.

"You wanna talk about him?" Simone asked gently, eyes on the fire.

Nia didn't answer right away. Just let the flames dance for a bit before she spoke.

"He pulled back."

"I figured."

"He said he needed space. Time to think."

Simone hummed. "Men love to think when things get too good."

Nia chuckled but it was quiet, almost tired. "I wasn't trying to rush him. I wasn't asking for anything he hadn't already started giving."

Simone nodded. "That's the thing. You weren't asking for too much. You were just being seen. And sometimes, that's enough to shake a man."

"I won't chase him," Nia said. "But I also don't want to shut the door."

"You didn't," Simone said. "You left the door open, Nia. But you didn't leave yourself out in the cold."

That landed.

Hard.

Nia stared into the fire for a long moment. Then: "I've worked too damn hard to build this peace. I'm not letting someone else's fear make me question my readiness."

Simone smiled, wide and proud. "Say that again for the women in the back."

Nia exhaled. "I'm not afraid of love. I just don't want to have to dim my light to earn it."

"And you won't have to," Simone said, leaning over to clink their glasses. "Because the man who's really meant for you? He won't be scared of your fullness. He'll be thirsty for it."

They both laughed, the sound easy and healing under the night sky.

"You think he'll come back?" Nia asked quietly.

Simone sipped, then said, "I don't know. But if he does, he'll have to come back clear. Not halfway. Not apologizing for needing time. But choosing you. Fully."

Nia nodded.

She didn't feel broken.

She felt ready.

And sometimes, that was the bravest thing of all.

Chapter 20

Dressed to Be Desired

The community center's annual fundraiser was buzzing. Laughter echoing under strings of fairy lights, kids darting between tables with cookies in hand, and the smell of cinnamon, barbecue, and warm cider wafting through the air.

Nia walked in like she belonged to every inch of the night.

Her olive green dress flowed around her like it had been stitched from the land itself. Her curls framed her face just right, her skin catching the soft glow of the lights. She didn't wear it like armor. She wore it like intention, ease, power, and grace.

She wasn't dressed to be noticed.

She was dressed to be remembered.

And someone was remembering.

Eli spotted her the moment he walked in. It felt like the whole room narrowed, like everything else dimmed except the woman standing across it.

She didn't smile when she saw him.

She didn't frown either.

She just looked, and in that look was every question he knew he had to answer.

He crossed the room slowly, stopping just in front of her with a breath that sounded a lot like surrender.

"You look like something a man should have the courage to hold," he said, voice low, steady.

Nia arched a brow, one corner of her mouth curving. "That's a pretty sentence, Eli. But I'm not here for poetry."

"I know."

Her eyes searched his. "Are you sure you're ready for this? For whatever this could be?"

He nodded once. "I am."

"I'm not doing the push-pull thing," she said, still steady, still soft. "We're too old for that. I've worked too hard to build this peace. If you come into my space, into my heart… you stay, or you don't come at all."

"I hear you," he said. "And I agree."

Her voice was calm, but her words had weight. "Do you even know what you want, Eli? And if you do… how do you know now? What changed?"

He stepped closer, not so much reaching for her as standing with full presence. "What changed is… I realized I already had what I was looking for. I just didn't believe I deserved it yet. So I pulled back not because I didn't want you, but because I didn't want to hurt something real by showing up halfway."

He paused, his voice dropping lower. "But the truth is, not choosing you? That felt worse."

Nia held his gaze, expression unreadable, but her shoulders had softened, just a little.

"I want the slow mornings," he continued. "The porch talks. The messy days. The nights where we don't say much and still say everything. I want the quiet, everyday parts of your life not just the easy ones."

He took one more step, now fully in her space.

"I'm not here with flowers and promises I can't keep. I'm here with intention. With clarity. And with a whole heart that wants to love you in a way that feels like breath, not pressure."

The music behind them shifted a soft, slow tune with just enough swing to make the couples nearby start to sway.

Nia exhaled, slow and deep, something settling in her chest.

"That's a start," she said. "But know this, if we do this, it's not casual. It's not background noise. It's... real."

"I wouldn't want it any other way," he said.

A beat passed between them.

Then Eli held out his hand.

"Can we pick up where we left off," he said, that easy smile playing at his lips, "keep dancing with me?"

She didn't rush.

But when she slipped her hand into his, it was steady.

And when he pulled her close, her head fit right where it belonged—just beneath his chin, right above his heartbeat.

They danced.

Not like strangers trying to impress each other.

Not like lovers trying to prove something.

But like a man who had learned the hard way what mattered.

And a woman who had finally made peace with being fully herself.

Eli pulled her in close, not just a brush of touch, but a firm, grounding embrace. One that said I'm here. One that said I see you.

She rested her cheek against his chest, feeling the steady rhythm of his heart.

He bent his head, lips brushing the curve of her ear. "I choose you," he whispered, voice thick with everything he meant. "And I won't lose sight of that again."

Nia closed her eyes, letting the words sink past skin, down to bone.

This time, she didn't just feel wanted.

She felt claimed, not as a possession, but as a promise.

And in that moment, wrapped in his arms, she knew:

They weren't starting over.

They were starting right.

Chapter 21

In Each Other's Space

Nia moved through the kitchen with a lightness she hadn't felt in weeks.

It wasn't butterflies; she was too grown for that, but something like a humming in her chest, steady and low. A sense of ease. Of direction.

He'd come back with clarity. With words that matched his actions. And that mattered.

At the fundraiser, when Eli had looked at her like she was the only woman in the room and said, "I'm not pretending I don't want you anymore," something in her settled. Not because she needed him to choose her; she was already whole. But because being chosen by someone who sees you? That sweetness hit different.

She sliced the last of the avocado just as she heard his truck crunch over the gravel. Junie's tail started wagging before the door even opened.

He gave a few quick taps on the door before walking in, holding a small bunch of wildflowers in one hand and that same soft look in his eyes.

"You still glowing from the other night," he said, pressing a kiss to her cheek.

Nia smiled, taking the flowers. "You still saying all the right things."

"I'm just telling the truth."

They fell into an easy rhythm.

He followed her into the kitchen, brushing past her intentionally, hand at the small of her back, fingers grazing her waist.

"You trying to distract me?" she asked, raising a brow.

Eli leaned in, lips just grazing her neck. "Am I succeeding?"

She didn't answer, just handed him the spatula with a knowing look.

They moved around each other like breath and heartbeat, close, warm, and familiar. He'd reach around her to grab a plate, let his hand slide across the curve of her hip. She'd pass him a fork, her fingers lingering just a little longer than necessary.

The tension wasn't heavy. It was delicious.

After breakfast, they took a walk along the ridge trail behind the property. Junie raced ahead, tail high like she owned the land. Eli reached for Nia's hand, fingers lacing easily through hers.

"You been in my head since that dance," he said quietly.

Nia looked over at him. "Good thoughts?"

He stopped walking, tugged her gently closer. "Real thoughts."

He kissed her, slow, sweet, with just enough pressure to remind her what they were building.

When they pulled apart, her forehead rested against his.

"I like us like this," she whispered. "Aligned. Uncomplicated."

He smiled. "I do too. And I'll do my part to keep it that way."

Back at the house, they sat on the porch sipping cold drinks,

Junie asleep at their feet.

Eli reached for the book he'd brought and opened it, but his hand found her thigh instead just above the knee. His thumb made small, slow circles, absent-minded but firm. Familiar.

She didn't stop him.

Didn't need to.

She leaned into it, let her head rest on his shoulder.

They didn't need to talk every minute. This, the warmth, the presence, the mutual wanting—was enough.

Later, when he stood to leave, he kissed her once on the mouth and once on the shoulder, just under the strap of her tank top.

"Same time tomorrow?" he asked, already knowing the answer.

She smiled, that slow, knowing smile of hers,

and gave a slight nod.

"'Night, Eli. Sleep well."

She started to turn, then glanced over her shoulder.

"Dream of me."

He let out a low, quiet growl, more rumble than sound, and stepped back slowly.

"That's all I do lately."

Their eyes held for just a moment longer. Heat, promise, and something real simmering beneath it all, before she slipped inside.

Chapter 22

A Little Heat, A Lot of Intention

The sun was sliding low when Eli showed up with that now-familiar knock-knock-push rhythm.

Nia had just finished her shower, a long sundress clinging to damp skin and curling tendrils framing her face like soft punctuation marks. She didn't rush to meet him at the door. She wanted to see if he'd find his way.

He did.

"Hey," he said softly when he spotted her, already slipping off his boots at the threshold like he belonged.

"Hey, yourself," she said, moving toward him slow and deliberate. "I wasn't expecting you this early."

"You sounded a little tired when we talked earlier," he said, brushing his fingers lightly along her arm as she passed. "Figured you could use some company."

That touch sparked something, not just between her shoulder and spine, but deeper. She could feel the want living right under her skin.

He followed her into the kitchen. She poured two glasses of tea, handing him one.

"You're dangerous," she said with a soft smirk.

He leaned against the counter. "How so?"

"You keep showing up just when I need you. That kind of timing makes a woman believe in fate."

He set his glass down and closed the space between them, hand resting on her hip like it had every right.

"I'm not trying to make you believe in fate," he murmured, brushing his lips against hers. "I'm trying to make you believe in me."

The kiss deepened before either of them fully decided it should.

Nia's hands slid up his chest, fingers curling into the collar of his shirt. His hands found her waist, then her back, pulling her just close enough to feel the heat but not quite enough to lose control.

When they finally broke apart, Nia stayed close, her breath just a little uneven.

"I want you," she said, voice low. "And you know that."

"I do," he replied, his hands still resting against the small of her back. "Trust me, the feeling is mutual."

"But this?" she said, tilting her chin. "I don't do halfway. I don't do 'we'll see.' If we cross that line... I need to know you're in."

Eli nodded slowly, his forehead resting gently against hers.

"You'll never have to question that with me ever again," he said. "This isn't a convenience thing. It's not a late-night craving. It's you, Nia. Daylight, peace, roots-deep you."

She closed her eyes for a second, grounding herself in that moment, in his steadiness, in her own.

"Okay," she whispered.

But she didn't take his hand to lead him to the bedroom just yet.

Instead, they sat down on the couch, bodies still humming, legs touching, hands never fully apart.

The fire was there, real and ready.

But so was the respect.

And when she leaned into his side, her fingers resting lightly on his chest, she let them drift—slow, curious—downward toward his stomach.

Does this man have six-pack abs?

She smiled to herself. I do love a man who takes care of himself.

It wasn't a tease. It was a quiet claim.

It was her way of learning him, of saying I see you. I feel you.

He drew in a breath, subtle but sharp, as if her touch caught him off guard in the best way.

He exhaled slow, like her touch had reached someplace deeper than skin.

Then, without hesitation, his arm slid around her waist and pulled her in firm, sure.

And when his mouth found hers, it wasn't soft or tentative.

It was a kiss that spoke of every moment he'd held back.

Slow, deep, and full of promise.

The kind of kiss that said he meant it.

"You keep touching me like that," he murmured, voice low and rough, "and I'm gonna forget we're taking this slow."

She smiled against his chest, fingers still resting over his heart.

"Then don't forget. Just… remember why."

He held her tighter.

And in that heat, wrapped in the steady rhythm of something real, they both knew it wasn't just desire.

It was a decision.

And that made all the difference.

Chapter 23

Driving to Something More

The kiss hadn't been planned.

But then again, neither was this connection, not like this.

And yet here they were.

After that night at her place, Nia found herself walking a little lighter. Not because she was falling but because she was finally letting go of the idea that love had to come with a warning label.

Eli hadn't pressed for more.

But the look in his eyes when she'd leaned back, breathless and still holding onto his shirt?

It said everything.

That he wanted her.

That he could wait.

That the wanting didn't diminish the respect.

And that stuck with her.

Meanwhile...

Eli had been pacing for the better part of an hour.

Not out of nerves but anticipation.

Something shifted that night when she touched him.

Not just her fingers on his chest, tracing slowly down like she was trying to memorize him but the way she looked at him afterward, like she saw all of him and didn't flinch.

He couldn't stop thinking about that smile. That slow, flirty "dream of me" smile.

And he had.

Every night since.

So when she'd said she'd come over this evening, something in him settled.

Like maybe, just maybe, they were both ready to cross whatever quiet line stood between "getting to know you" and being known.

Now, a few days later, she was on her way to his house, not because they needed to define anything, but because she wanted to.

To see him in his space.

To feel what it was like to move a little closer without losing herself.

The drive to Eli's place wasn't far, but it gave Nia just enough time to think.

He hadn't said much when he invited her, just that he was grilling and wanted her to see the place. But something about his voice had held a quiet edge, like he was letting her in a little deeper than usual.

She pulled up to find his dog, Harley, a lazy old hound mix, stretched out in the driveway like he owned the land. Junie, perched in the passenger seat beside her, perked up with a soft whine.

"Be cool, sweet girl," Nia whispered with a grin. "We're guests."

Eli met her at the door with two beers and a slow smile. He looked good. Easy jeans, a soft black T-shirt, and that same low hum of confidence that always felt earned, never forced.

"You brought her," he said, nodding to Junie as she jumped out and sniffed her way over to Harley.

"Thought they might get along," Nia said. "Like their people."

He laughed and stepped aside, letting her in.

The house was warm. Lived-in. Not messy, not overly neat. There were books everywhere—stacked on tables, on the floor, even on the windowsill next to a plant that looked half-alive and fully stubborn.

"You actually read all of these?" she asked, trailing her fingers along a spine.

"Most of them," he said. "Some I keep around because they remind me of where I was when I bought them."

The kitchen smelled like garlic and thyme. A pan of roasted sweet potatoes sat cooling on the stove, and he had fish marinating in a glass bowl beside a loaf of bread he clearly hadn't baked but proudly displayed anyway.

"You cook and you read?" she teased.

"I'm a man of depth," he said with mock seriousness, pulling out a chair for her. "Sit. Let me feed you."

As they ate, Nia noticed the photos on the mantle. One of Eli and his daughter when she was young, both of them laughing in the middle of a snowball fight. A couple of framed Polaroids of fishing trips, a candid shot of him mid-laugh, holding up a slice of watermelon like it was a trophy.

He noticed her looking.

"She says I always smiled bigger when I wasn't trying," he said.

"She's right."

There was a quiet beat between them.

"You talk about her with ease," Nia said. "Seems like you have a great relationship."

"We do. She's a good kid," he said. "And she likes you."

Nia smiled softly. "Good. Because I like her too."

They moved to the couch, their plates empty and their bodies comfortably full. The sun was dipping now, soft amber light filtering in through the blinds.

Eli reached under the coffee table and pulled out a slim black notebook.

"I wrote something," he said, not quite looking at her. "After that week we didn't talk."

He handed it over.

Nia opened to a page marked with a dog-ear. Inside, in his handwriting, neat but a little uneven, was a short entry:

"She doesn't make me feel like I have to be anything. Just present. And that's the scariest part—because when you're seen that clearly, you can't hide. But God... I don't want to hide from her."

She read it twice. Then again, slower.

"I didn't write it to impress you," he said. "I just wanted to remember how I felt in that space. Afraid. But sure."

She closed the notebook and sat it in her lap, hand sliding across his.

"I don't need a man who never feels fear," she said, her voice calm but steady. "I need a man who doesn't let it make decisions for him."

She reached for his hand, lacing her fingers through his.

"Thank you for sharing this with me."

There was no judgment in her eyes, only tenderness.

And that quiet kind of strength that made a man feel safe enough to stay open.

Eli turned to her, eyes steady, voice low.

"Thank you... for giving me the space to be vulnerable."

Nia held his gaze, something warm blooming in her chest.

A man who could show vulnerability and still stand in his strength?

Sexy as hell.

She didn't say it out loud.

She didn't have to.

The way her fingers curled a little tighter around his told him everything he needed to know.

She leaned in, kissing him once—slow, sweet, solid.

And when they finally settled into the couch, legs tangled, her head on his chest, his hand on her thigh, it wasn't passion pulling them forward. It was intimacy.

And that?

That was everything.

Chapter 24

The First Time

The rain had started just after sunset. Light at first, then steady, wrapping the evening in a hush.

Nia stood at the sliding door in Eli's living room, watching droplets gather on the glass. Her body was still warm from the wine, her heart even warmer from the night they'd shared. Full of small talk, full plates, and slow touches that lingered just a little longer than before.

Eli came up behind her without a word, sliding his arms around her waist, his chin finding the curve of her shoulder like he'd done it a hundred times.

"You good?" he asked softly, voice low and lined with heat.

She didn't answer right away. Just leaned back into him and let the moment stretch.

"I'm better than good," she finally whispered.

He turned her gently, and when their eyes met, there was a knowing. They were both ready to deepen their connection, their intimacy.

His fingers skimmed the strap of her dress, tracing the line from her shoulder to her collarbone. She watched him, calm and steady, as he kissed that spot. Then another. Then lower.

By the time they made it to the bedroom, they were both barefoot, breathless, and smiling.

Eli took his time.

He didn't just undress her—he unwrapped her.

Slowly. Softly. Like a gift.

Nia didn't cover up. Didn't hide her stretch marks or scars or the places where softness lived. She let him see all of her and in his eyes, she saw nothing but hunger and awe.

"You are so damn beautiful," he murmured, hand resting at the dip of her waist. "Do you even know?"

She swallowed hard. "Feel free to keep telling me."

They kissed again. Deeper now, lips parting, breath catching.

Eli laid her back against the sheets like she was something sacred.

His hands moved over her slowly, reverently—tracing every curve like a map he never wanted to stop exploring.

Every sigh, every whispered yes that slipped from her lips only deepened his hunger.

Not just to have her—

But to know her.

When he finally entered her, it wasn't fast. It wasn't rough.

It was home.

And when their rhythm found its pace, slow, rising, full—Nia let herself feel everything.

The intimacy. The pleasure.

The way her body responded to his, like they had always known each other.

They moved together easily, effortlessly, like two halves of a song finally meeting in the same key.

Each touch, each breath, each slow thrust felt like a quiet yes her soul had been waiting to say.

She felt full of him, not just physically, but emotionally.

Filled in all the places that had once felt forgotten.

Eli kissed her neck, then her shoulder, then the inside of her wrist, slow and reverent, like he was still learning her by heart.

And even in the middle of that stillness, he could feel it rising again, the craving, the pull.

It wasn't just desire. It was need.

Not rushed, but constant. Building.

And then, together, they came undone.

A shared breath. A held moan. A moment suspended in heat and heartbeat.

The release came like a wave, washing over them both, not just of need, but of all the things they'd held back.

Past heartache. Loneliness. Hope.

His name caught on her lips like a prayer.

Her body arched into his as he buried his face in the curve of her neck, holding her close, grounding them in something that felt holy.

For a long time, neither of them moved.

Not because they were too tired, but because they didn't want to lose that moment.

That stillness. That knowing.

That quiet afterglow that whispered, you are not alone anymore.

They just stayed wrapped around each other, the storm outside echoing the quiet thunder of her heartbeat.

They lay there breathless, still tingling from the fire they'd just made, not just heat, but connection. Deep, intentional, soul-level intimacy.

Eli shifted slightly, then cupped her face, pulling her in for a kiss that was slow and deep, sure. The kind of kiss that sealed something.

Nia exhaled into it, her fingers brushing the edge of his jaw before letting go.

They curled into each other beneath the sheets, her back to his chest, his arm wrapped tight around her waist like a vow.

He pressed his lips to the back of her neck, voice barely a whisper against her skin.

"You know I'm never letting you go... right?"

Nia didn't answer with words; she just let her hand slide over his and held on as her breath slowed.

And just like that, with the rain still falling soft outside, she drifted off in his arms.

She felt safe. She felt loved.

Chapter 25

Defining Forever

The next morning arrived quiet and golden, sunlight easing through the bedroom blinds in soft strips.

Nia stirred first, blinking slowly as her body remembered the night before. The heat of it, the gentleness, the way her name sounded on Eli's lips like something sacred.

He was still behind her, one arm draped over her waist, his breath steady against her shoulder. She didn't move, didn't rush. Just listened.

And felt.

Safe. Wanted. Whole.

"Morning," he murmured, voice thick with sleep.

"Hey," she said softly, smiling into the pillow.

He kissed the back of her shoulder, then rested his forehead there. "How you feelin'?"

She rolled onto her back to face him, her eyes searching his. "Good. Great," she said, with a smile.

"Same," as he gave her a gentle squeeze.

They lay there in the hush, no need to fill the air with fluff.

Until Nia spoke, voice even and sure. "So... what now?"

He didn't flinch. Didn't stall.

He propped himself up on one elbow, eyes steady. "We're building something. Slow. Intentional. Honest."

She nodded. "And what does that look like... practically?"

Eli reached for her hand, threading his fingers through hers.

"It looks like choosing each other every day," he said. "Showing up. Talking when it's hard. Laughing when it's easy. Loving without shrinking."

Nia raised an eyebrow, playful. "You been reading my coaching notes?"

"I've been watching you," he said. "Learning from you."

She softened, her thumb brushing over his knuckles.

"I don't want to lose myself," she said quietly. "I've done that before. I want to be us, but I still need to be me."

"I wouldn't want it any other way," he said. "I love your fire, your freedom, your damn solitude. I just want to be the man who gets to sit beside all of that and not dim a single part of it."

A long pause.

Then Nia smiled, and it was deep, not the flirty one, not the polite one. The kind of smile that came from truth.

"Alright then," she said. "We keep our own homes. Our own rhythms. But we make space for each other, real space."

Eli nodded. "Done."

"And I want joy," she added, "not just comfort. Passion. Play. Prayer. All of it."

"You'll have all of it," he said. "You already do."

He kissed her then, soft and unhurried, like the promise it was.

Later, they sat on the porch, coffee mugs in hand, legs touching beneath the blanket. Junie and Harley curled up at their feet, the sky wide and blue above them.

There was no official title.

No big announcement.

Just a choice made clear—two people, whole on their own, choosing to walk forward together.

Not perfect.

Not performative.

Just real.

Rooted.

And just beginning.

Chapter 26

Spill the Tea

Tasha was elbow-deep in a solar panel cleaning when Nia wandered over with two bottles of cold hibiscus water and a smirk that said "I've got a secret."

Tasha didn't even look up.

"Girl, you are floating'. Don't even try to act normal."

Nia laughed and handed her a bottle. "I am not floating."

"You floated your little barefoot self out of Eli's truck yesterday like you were walking on warm clouds and holy promises," Tasha teased, wiping sweat from her brow. "Now spill it."

Nia leaned back against the wooden post of the shed, sipping slowly. "It was... beautiful."

Tasha raised an eyebrow and gave her a look.

Nia grinned. "Okay fine, it was amazing. Respectful. Intentional. Intimate."

Tasha grunted. "That's sweet. But girl, I said spill it. You know what I mean."

Nia blinked, then narrowed her eyes. "You are not about to make me talk about—"

"Oh, I am. Is he working with something or not? Be honest."

"Tasha!"

Tasha leaned in, wide-eyed and waiting. "Look, I've built houses, fixed pipes, and installed systems, but I still need a man that can lay some good foundation, if you know what I'm saying."

Nia dissolved into laughter, fanning herself with her hand. "You are ridiculous."

"But am I wrong?"

Nia bit her lip, cheeks warming, but she didn't look away.

"He took his time," she said, her voice low and a little breathy. "Made me feel like the only woman on earth. And let's just say…"— she leaned in with a wicked little grin—"the man knows exactly what to do with his hands."

Tasha's eyes widened. "Girl—!"

Nia laughed. "Is that what you wanted to hear?"

Tasha let out a whistle. "Uh huh. I knew that man had strong-hands energy. Probably got that linger stroke, not that rush job."

"Tasha!"

"I'm just sayin'. I like to know what's in the blueprint before I invest emotionally."

They laughed harder now, Junie trotting up to investigate the fuss.

Once the giggles died down, Tasha tossed her rag onto the bench and leaned back, eyes a little softer now.

"I'm happy for you," she said, more sincere. "You've been through it. Quiet about it too. But you told me how you lost pieces of yourself for a long time. And now… you're back."

Nia nodded, her voice quieter. "I feel back. Not because of him, but… because I was ready. And he just showed up at the right moment."

"You built the space. And now it's being filled with someone who actually sees the value of it. That's what makes it beautiful."

Nia exhaled. "I was scared I wouldn't want again. But I do. And that's the biggest surprise."

Tasha smiled. "Wanting again means you're alive. But being selective?" She tapped her temple. "That's the wisdom part."

They clinked bottles, their laughter now replaced with a soft, shared peace.

As the sun arched higher in the sky, the two women stood in the middle of land they were shaping with their own hands, surrounded by trees, possibilities, and one big juicy secret that Nia would definitely get grilled about again soon.

Chapter 27

Sweet Tea and Soft Truths

The sun was low and syrupy, casting golden light across the land as Simone arranged a few throw pillows around the fire pit. She did everything with intention; even outdoor seating had to feel like a welcome hug.

Nia showed up barefoot, still in her linen wrap dress from earlier, curls slightly wild from the breeze and whatever sweet kiss Eli had pressed on her before she slipped away for girls' time.

"Well look at you," Simone said with a raised brow and a slow smile. "You glowing like somebody been touched by the Lord and a good man."

Nia laughed, flopping down into one of the cushioned chairs. "It's the sunset. That's all."

"Mmmhmm," Simone said, handing her a glass of her famous peach sweet tea. "I've seen a lotta sunsets, baby. That glow is inner."

Nia sipped and settled in, the warmth of the fire licking gently at her toes.

"You doing alright?" Simone asked after a few quiet sips. "With all this... heart-opening business?"

Nia paused. "I am. It's not overwhelming. It's soft. Steady. He shows up like he said he would."

Simone smiled into her glass. "Consistency is underrated, huh?"

"Very," Nia nodded. "It's the difference between guessing and knowing."

Simone leaned forward, poking the fire just enough to let it crackle again.

"Let me tell you something," she said, eyes fixed on the flame. "For years, I thought I was too much—too loud, too hopeful, too full of ideas and sunshine. Men would show up, smile in my light, and then say it was 'a lot' once it started to shine in their shadow."

Nia's voice was quiet but certain. "That's not 'too much.' That's power."

"I realized that, eventually. I stopped trying to dim," Simone continued, sitting back. "I just built a life bright enough for me. But watching you... this thing with Eli? It reminds me that maybe the right man doesn't need me to tone anything down. He'll just wear sunglasses and keep up."

Nia reached over and squeezed her hand. "He's out there, Simone. Some man with good credit, strong arms, and a deep appreciation for a southern woman who knows her worth and makes a mean skillet cornbread."

They both laughed, the tension melting into the stars above them.

Simone looked at her with warmth. "You know, I admire you, Nia. You're letting yourself have this joy. You're not side-eyeing it, or second-guessing it. You're receiving it. That's powerful."

"It's new," Nia admitted. "But it feels right. Like something I planted a long time ago is finally blooming."

"Well," Simone said, raising her glass again, "here's to love, soft when it needs to be, strong when it counts, and always on your level."

They clinked glasses, Junie snoring softly at their feet, and the fire warming the night around them.

In that moment, with the crickets singing and their hearts light, Nia felt it deep in her chest:

This wasn't a love story she was waiting for.

This was one she was living.

Chapter 28

The Ring

Nia pulled up to Eli's place just as the sky turned that velvety blue that only happens right after sunset. The porch lights were on, and she could hear an old jazz record humming low through the windows.

Junie trotted ahead like she knew the place by heart.

Eli opened the door before she could knock. He looked relaxed in his soft t-shirt and cargo pants, barefoot. There was a warmth in his eyes that made her stomach flip, even now.

"I was just about to text you," he said, stepping aside. "Dinner's almost ready."

She kissed him on the cheek as she passed. "You're getting real domestic."

"You bring that out of me."

The dining table was set simply. Linen napkins, mismatched candles, two plates of roasted vegetables, grilled salmon, and cornbread in the cast iron like a man who understood Southern hospitality.

They ate slow, hands brushing now and then, conversation light.

But Nia could feel something else under the surface; there was a hum between them. Eli kept glancing toward the sideboard drawer. Something was coming.

After they cleared the dishes and poured tea, he stood and walked to the drawer, pulling out a small velvet pouch. No box. No bow. Just simple and real.

He came back and sat beside her on the couch.

"I've been thinking about this a lot," he said, holding the pouch in one hand, the other resting over hers. "Not about a proposal. Not about changing your name or mailing off papers. Just this…"

He opened it and slid the ring into her palm. It was delicate, elegant, and earthy. A thin gold band with a tiny raw garnet at the center, deep and red like the soil she planted in every day.

She stared at it, silent, moved.

"This ring isn't a claim," he said. "It's a reminder. That I see you. That I choose you. That I'm not going anywhere, not when it's easy, not when it's hard. You're mine… because you want to be. Not because you have to be."

Nia swallowed hard, her fingers curling around the ring.

"I love you," he added quietly. "I've known it for a while now. I just wanted to say it when I had something real to hand you too."

She looked up at him, eyes shining, throat thick with emotion, and whispered back, "I love you too."

He let out the softest breath, like he'd been holding it all night.

"Say it again," he murmured.

"I love you," she said, louder now, with that little half-smile she saved just for him. "And I'll wear this. Not because I need the world to know. But because I want you to know."

He slipped the ring onto her finger. It was light, simple, and stunning, then looked up at her like she was the only thing that had ever made sense.

"I love you," he said again, voice thick, low. "I've been holding it in, but not anymore. I love you, Nia. With intention. With clarity."

Nia leaned forward, heart thundering. "I love you too, Eli. I love how you see me. I love who I am when I'm with you. I feel... chosen. Not claimed. At peace."

That was all it took.

Eli's hand slid to the back of her neck, his mouth finding hers with a hunger that had been simmering since the day they met. This wasn't slow or hesitant; it was all-in. Tongues tangled, bodies pulled tight. The tea went cold on the coffee table, forgotten.

He stood, scooped her into his arms, and carried her to the bedroom, kissing the edge of her jaw the whole way there.

"I need you," he growled against her collarbone.

"I'm yours," she breathed, fingers already tugging at the hem of his shirt. "Now show me."

Clothes were peeled away in a blur of moans and rushed hands. Her back hit the sheets and he followed, tracing every inch of her like he couldn't believe she was real.

"God, you're beautiful," he said, his voice rough. "Do you even know what you do to me?"

"Let me show you what you do to me," she said, flipping them with a grin that was all confidence, curves, and fire.

They moved together like music, heat building, lips everywhere, his hands gripping her thighs. She rode him slow, then faster, until they were gasping, lost in the rhythm of what they'd created.

And when they finally let go together it was with her name on his lips, and his body wrapped around hers like he couldn't stand the thought of distance.

He didn't pull away.

He didn't get up.

He just held her close, pressing kisses into her shoulder as her breath slowed.

His fingers brushed over the ring still glinting on her hand.

"You're mine," he whispered, his voice soft now. "And I'm yours."

Nia kissed him full on the mouth, and smiled against his lips.

"I know."

And just like that, wrapped in heat, promise, and the kind of love that only comes from seeing and being seen, they drifted off, bodies tangled and futures sealed.

Chapter 29

Planning Forever

It had been a few weeks since Eli slipped the ring on Nia's finger, but the moment still lingered in her bones like music after the last note. A soft, sweet humming coursed through her whole body.

She hadn't taken the ring off once. Not while planting tomatoes. Not while washing dishes. Not even when soaking in the clawfoot tub she'd worked so hard to restore. It wasn't just a ring; it was a reminder: she was loved. Freely. Fiercely. Fully.

Telling the girls had been a moment all its own.

Tasha screamed.

Simone cried.

And Junie barked like she knew her mama was about to be even more spoiled.

They didn't ask if a wedding was coming. They didn't question if this love was real. They just wrapped Nia up in their arms and called it what it was, a win for all of them.

"Okay," Simone had said, wiping her eyes with one hand and already pulling out her notes app with the other. "So we're doing this right. Commitment celebration. Elegant, intimate, and full of good food."

"I didn't say we were—"

Simone waved her off. "You've already said yes to the man. Don't you dare say no to the moment."

Nia had laughed, blushing and biting back tears of her own. Because the truth was... she wanted it. Not a wedding. Not a spectacle. Just something to mark this chapter. To honor what they were building, not just as a couple, but as a community.

Now, two weeks out from the big day, the planning was in full swing.

Tasha was handling the setup—clearing space beneath the giant oak tree near the edge of the property, mapping out seating, and figuring out how to string lights from the low-hanging branches without falling off the ladder. Again.

"I'm thinking mismatched chairs and benches," she said, scribbling in her sketchbook. "Rustic but cozy. And maybe a draped arch, but nothing too... frilly."

Simone had already ordered the florals. Big bunches of wildflowers, eucalyptus, and a few sprigs of dried lavender. "It needs to smell like peace and look like joy," she'd said, tapping through photos on her phone like a woman possessed. "Also, I'm wearing gold. I don't care what y'all do."

Eli's daughter, Maya, had offered to help with food and music, a playlist of soul classics and slow jams that felt like long walks and Sunday mornings.

Even Harley, Eli's big lazy dog, had a role, wearing a simple collar of green sprigs and sunflowers to match Junie's little flower crown.

And Nia?

She was keeping things simple.

She'd walk to the oak tree barefoot, wearing a soft ivory dress she'd found tucked in a bin of vintage clothes she hadn't unpacked since moving from Illinois. No veil. No bouquet. Just her ring, her people, and her heart wide open.

But in the quiet moments, early morning tea, or late-night journaling, she could feel the emotions rising like a tide.

Not nerves.

Not doubt.

Just gratitude.

She was doing this her way—after years of pouring into others, shrinking to fit, and waiting for the "right" moment. Now she stood tall in the life she built with her hands and her healing.

And Eli?

He showed up every step of the way. Helping where needed. Giving space where necessary. Loving her through it all.

"I just want you to feel celebrated," he'd said one night as they sat beneath the stars.

"I already do," she replied.

But now, with candles being ordered, playlists getting finalized, and her best friends scheming over seating charts and signature drinks, Nia knew:

She was about to be honored.

Fully.

Joyfully.

And in front of the people who knew her story and still chose to clap the loudest.

Chapter 30

The Commitment

Eli stood in front of the bathroom mirror, adjusting the cuffs of his light linen shirt for the third time. The buttons were off by one, again. He laughed softly under his breath and shook his head.

"Get it together, old man," he muttered, but the smile on his face said otherwise.

It had been a long time since he'd felt this kind of nervous, not anxious or unsure. Just full. Like his chest couldn't quite hold the depth of what today meant.

He never thought he'd find love again. And not just love, but find her. Nia, with her wild curls and sharp mind and hands always in the soil. She was sunlight and steadiness. And somehow, she'd said yes—to him, to this, to now.

"You ready?" Maya's voice floated in from the hallway.

Eli turned just as his daughter stepped into the room, wearing a sage green dress and a soft smile.

"You look beautiful," he said, eyes shining.

"Thanks, Dad." She walked over, fixing his collar. "You look... smitten."

Eli chuckled. "I am. More than I ever thought I could be again."

Maya stepped back and studied him. "I'm happy for you. For both of you."

There was a beat of quiet, not awkward, just tender.

"I wasn't sure how you'd feel," he said honestly. "Me finding someone again."

"I wondered too," she admitted. "But then I met her. And I got it. She's warm. She listens. She makes you laugh, like real belly laugh. And she makes you softer."

Eli swallowed hard.

"She loves you, Dad. Like... all of you. That's rare. And I'm proud to stand beside you today."

Harley thudded his big body against the hallway wall like he was ready to go, tail wagging in wide, lazy arcs.

Maya laughed. "Okay, Harley's definitely ready."

Eli gave one last glance in the mirror, exhaled, and nodded.

"Let's go get our girl."

The clearing beneath the old oak tree had been transformed into something quietly magical. String lights swayed gently overhead, catching the breeze like whispers. Wildflowers danced in mason jars down the center aisle, and mismatched chairs held the people who loved Nia and Eli most.

Junie wore her flower crown proudly, perched next to Tasha and Simone who were both dressed in their own perfect versions of occasion-ready. Tasha rocked a fitted jumpsuit with sandals. Simone wore gold, as promised, and had already cried twice—and the ceremony hadn't even started.

And then Nia appeared.

Barefoot. Glowing. The ivory dress flowing like it had been made just for her.

She didn't rush. Didn't pretend to float.

She walked like a woman grounded with each step its own quiet vow.

Eli's breath caught when he saw her.

Maya squeezed his arm, eyes glistening.

As Nia reached the front, Junie let out a soft bark, like she knew this was the moment. Harley sat beside her, patient and calm with the two dogs framing the scene like a blessing.

They didn't have an officiant. Just each other. And their words.

Eli took both of Nia's hands, eyes locked on hers.

"I don't need paperwork or tradition to know that I'm yours," he said. "I've been yours from the first day you challenged me without flinching, loved me without limits, and looked at me like I was still worth choosing. I promise to honor you, to support your joy, and to always—always—tell you how beautiful you are. Every day. Until my last breath."

Nia's throat tightened as she smiled through the tears.

"I don't want perfect," she said. "I want real. I want steady. I want mornings where we sit in silence and nights where we dance in the kitchen. I want your rough hands, your soft heart, and that steady look that tells me I'm safe. I promise to love you fully, freely, and without apology."

They slipped their hands back together—fingers interlocked like a signature.

Simone wiped her cheeks. Tasha smiled wide. Maya held her phone steady, capturing it all.

They kissed beneath the oak tree, the lights above them swaying like stars come down to witness it.

And when they turned to face their people, hands still clasped, the applause rang out like music.

The celebration that followed was full of laughter, hugs, good food, and plenty of barefoot dancing.

No titles were exchanged. No paperwork signed.

But everyone there knew:

Something sacred had taken root. Something only God could have orchestrated.

They weren't just witnessing a ceremony. They were witnessing love—in action and on purpose.

Epilogue

After the Vows

Three months later

The morning was quiet and peaceful.

A soft hum of bees moved lazily through the herb garden. A kettle whistled from the stove inside the tiny home. And Nia, still barefoot and wrapped in Eli's oversized flannel, moved slowly through the rows of basil and mint, gently pinching leaves between her fingers.

She looked out across the land. The oak tree still strung with lights, the handmade benches still tucked beneath it. Wildflowers had started to grow where their chairs had been, like the earth was holding on to the memory too.

Inside, Eli leaned against the doorway, coffee in hand, watching her.

He still couldn't believe it sometimes, that this woman, with her messy curls and dirt-kissed hands and open, steady heart, was his. Not because of a license or a label. But because every day since that moment under the tree, she had chosen him.

She turned and caught his gaze, a smile spreading slow across her face.

"You staring again, my love?" she teased.

"Every chance I get," he replied.

Junie was curled in her usual spot on the porch. Harley snored softly by the steps. The world felt full but not crowded. Busy, but never rushed.

Maya visited last weekend, bringing a big tin of blueberry muffins and an old quilt for their reading nook. Simone was busy launching their new digital newsletter — "Rooted Love & Living," she'd named it — and Tasha had started offering hands-on solar training classes for women in the county.

The land buzzed with life.

But here, in this quiet moment between chores and phone calls and laughter-filled dinners, Nia felt something deeper than happiness.

She felt peace.

Eli stepped down and joined her, wrapping an arm around her waist as they looked out across the trees.

"No big plans today?" he asked.

She leaned into him. "Nope. Just this."

They stood like that for a long while, coffee cooling in his hand, wind tugging gently at her robe.

And if anyone had passed by right then — neighbors, travelers, friends — they wouldn't have needed a sign or a sermon to understand what they were seeing.

They'd know.

Nia and Eli — yeah, they nailed it. And this? This was just the beginning of their love story in progress.

Sneak Peek

Book 2 - Tasha

Tasha came to the quiet hills of Kentucky for peace, not passion. But when a broad-shouldered local with a slow smile and hands that know exactly what they're doing walks into her life, she realizes settling down might mean letting things get deliciously out of control.

She came to the hills to plant roots. Not to fix her heart. Not to chase a dream. Just plant herself in one place and let a new life find her right where she is.

Tasha spent her childhood packing boxes and chasing her parents' next military post, always searching for a place that felt like hers. She found it with Marcus—until one tragic accident took him, their unborn child, and the future she'd been holding in both hands.

Anger. Guilt. Loneliness. She fought her way through them all —first in a self-defense class, then in a boxing ring, and, when that wasn't enough, on the spiciest corner of her favorite creator's OnlyFans page. Now she's fit, fierce, and—if she's honest—horny as hell.

Meeting Nia at a women's kayaking retreat led her to the hills of Kentucky, a tiny house community, and the quiet she craved. She brought her tools, her skills, and a promise to herself: this time, she'd stand firmly—on her need for passion.

But the peace she came for is about to get a little... louder. Because the one thing she never expected in these hills? A Kentucky man who can rock her world—and her bed.

About the Author

Antoinette T. Burson is a wedding officiant, tiny home dweller, and nature lover who believes love only deepens with time. A widow at 54, she's officiating small intimate weddings, living part-time in her cozy off-grid home, and writing stories that fill her cup. She hopes that her stories will help women rediscover joy, purpose, and passion. Nailed It: A Love Story in Progress is her debut romance—and a gentle reminder that it's never too late for a second chance at love.

Dear Reader

Thank You for sharing this chapter of love, growth, and the brave kind of self-discovery that happens when I let faith lead the way. Writing Nailed It: A Love Story in Progress has been part prayer, part dreaming, and part stepping into the woman I'm still becoming.

If this story touched you, reminded you of your own strength, or whispered to you that it's never too late to choose yourself again, then I'm grateful. My hope is that as you turn these final pages, you carry a little more courage, a little more softness, and a whole lot more faith into whatever comes next.

From my tiny house dreams to yours—thank you for reading.

With love, Antoinette